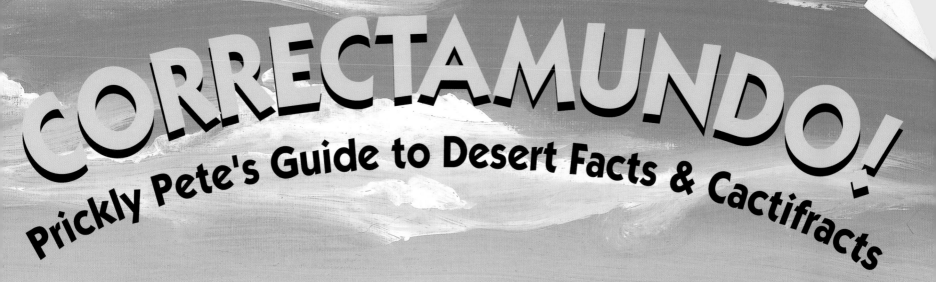

CORRECTAMUNDO!

Prickly Pete's Guide to Desert Facts & Cactifracts

by David Lazaroff   illustrations by Preston

From the Arizona-Sonora Desert Museum

Correctamundo!

Prickly Pete's Guide to Desert Facts & Cactifracts

Cactifracts???

To Cat —D.L.

To my mom and all other
lovers of horned toads. —P.N.

Acknowledgments

Many people helped put the fun in this book.
Special thanks to Steve Phillips at the Desert
Museum, and above all to the third grades at
Mazanita Elementary School in Tucson,
Arizona, for their great suggestions during
the 1999-2000 school year.

Sonya Connolly's class
Mary Engle's class
Kim Huffman's class
Donna Thomason's class
Martha Thomason's class

—D.L.

Text Copyright © 2001 by Arizona-Sonora Desert Museum
All rights reserved.

Illustrations Copyright © 2001 by Preston Neel
All rights reserved.

Design by Rudy J. Ramos, Rudy Ramos Design Studio
Printed in Hong Kong by Midas Printing
Published in the United States by Arizona-Sonora Desert Museum
2021 N. Kinney Road, Tucson, Arizona 85743
www.desertmuseum.org

This book is available at quantity discounts for educational, business, or sales promotional use.
For further information, please contact ARIZONA-SONORA DESERT MUSEUM PRESS
2021 N. Kinney Road, Tucson, AZ 85743 • (520) 883-3028

FIRST EDITION
ISBN 1-886679-17-7

Lazaroff, David Wentworth, 1948-
Correctamundo!: Prickly Pete's guide to desert facts and cactifracts / written by David Lazaroff;
illustrated by Preston Neel.— 1st ed.
p. cm.
ISBN 1-886679-17-7
1. Deserts—Miscellanea—Juvenile literature. 2. Desert animals—Miscellanea—Juvenile literature.
3. Desert Plants—Miscellanea—Juvenile literature. [1. Desert animals—Miscellanea. 2. Desert
Plants—Miscellanea.] I. Neel, Preston, ill. II. Title.

QH88.L42 2001
578.754—dc21   00-052598

AN ARIZONA-SONORA DESERT MUSEUM PRESS BOOK

Monster lizards! Poisonous plants! Creepy-crawlies at night!
You've heard some weird stuff about the desert, right? Guess what. Lots of it's true! The desert really is a pretty weird place.

But some of the weird stuff you hear about the desert isn't true at all. Even if it's on TV. Even if it's on the Internet. Even if your best friend's favorite uncle says so for sure!

What do we call something about the desert that's true?
A FACT!
(OK, *boring,* everybody knows that.)

But what should we call something about the desert that *isn't* true, even though lots of people think it is? How about...
A CACTIFRACT!
Can *you* tell a fact from a cactifract? Let's find out.

Lots of people think a desert tortoise can crawl right out of its shell.

What do *you* think?
FACT or CACTIFRACT?

If you said CACTIFRACT, YOU'RE TURTALLY AWESOME!

A tortoise's shell isn't a house he carries around! It's part of his body!

The outside of the shell is super-hard tortoise skin. It's made of the same stuff as your fingernails, only thicker and darker.

Inside that are flat bones with their edges stuck tight together. They make the shell super-strong!

The tortoise's ribs and backbone are attached to the flat bones. They're part of the shell, too!

A tortoise crawling out of its shell would be like *you* crawling out of your skin—and part of your skeleton! Want to try it? **Good luck!**

Lots of people think that when Gila monsters bite they won't let go.

What do *you* think?
FACT or CACTIFRACT?

If you said FACT, yikes!
YOU'RE MONSTROUSLY CORRECT!

But don't worry! Gila monsters aren't waiting in the desert to get you!

When a Gila monster sees you coming, usually it just stands still or hides under a bush. No problem!

If you get really close (*not* a great idea) it opens its big mouth *wide* and *hisses*. What's it telling you?

Right! Don't Mess With Me!

Now, let's say you poke that lizard or try to pick it up. BAD idea! *Then* it might chomp onto you! But are you going to do that?

A Gila monster needs its venom for the critters it eats. It doesn't want to waste it on you. You're much too big to swallow!

Speaking of lizards...

Lots of people think horny toads
shoot blood from their eyes.

What do *you* think?
FACT or CACTIFRACT?

If you said FACT,
LEAPING LIZARDS, you're RIGHT!

Wow! Squirt gun eyes! Here's what happens.

A hungry coyote spots a nice fat horny toad. Lunch time! He picks it up in his mouth. Right away the horny toad squirts blood into the coyote's mouth. Right away the coyote spits out the horny toad.

How come? Horny toad eye blood tastes *horrible* to members of the dog family. That's why horny toads mainly squirt coyotes, foxes, and dogs. Self defense!

Weird experiment time. Some scientists tasted horny toad eye blood. They found out it doesn't taste too bad to people. But you probably wouldn't want a horny toad for lunch, anyway!

Lots of people think a jumping cactus jumps.

What do *you* think?
FACT or CACTIFRACT?

If you said CACTIFRACT, CARTWHEELING CACTI, right AGAIN!

One day you're happily hiking along in the desert. Suddenly—**OUCH!** A piece of spiny cactus is stuck to your arm or your leg. How did it get there? It must have jumped onto you, right? Wrong!

A jumping cactus looks like a big bunch of spiny hot dogs stuck together end to end. These pieces come apart really easily. If you brush up against a jumping cactus—even just barely—a piece can break right off and stick onto you!

So unless you think it's cool to wear a cactus, always watch where you're going. And *never* back up in the desert without looking first!

Lots of people think javelinas (hav-uh-LEE-nuz) are wild desert pigs.

What do *you* think?
FACT or CACTIFRACT?

If you said CACTIFRACT,
PERFECT, PROFESSOR PORKOLOGIST!

Javelinas aren't pigs, they're peccaries! (Say PECK-uh-reez, professor.)

A peccary sure *looks* like a pig. You'd have to get real close to one to see what makes it different. You'd have to count its toes and its teeth. Don't try it!

Fortunately, there's a way to tell a javelina is a peccary without getting too close. Javelinas stink!

Every peccary has a little "scent gland" hidden under the fur on its back. A little gland with a giant smell! Pigs don't have one, peccaries do.

So if you're out in the desert and you smell something *really terrible,* don't be surprised. It could be peccary perfume! (Or maybe you just need a bath.)

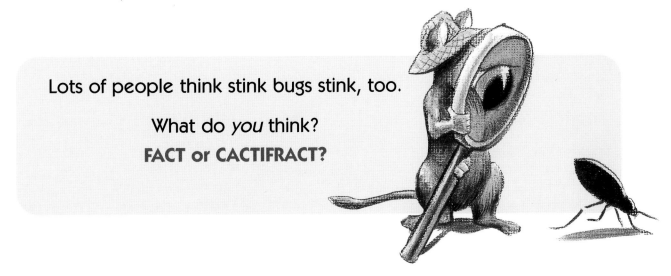

Lots of people think stink bugs stink, too.

What do *you* think?
FACT or CACTIFRACT?

If you said FACT, fabulous!
YOU'VE SNIFFED OUT THE TRUTH!

All over the world there are bugs that stink. (Aren't we lucky!) In the desert when people say "stink bug" they're talking about a weird little critter with a cool name—a pinacate beetle! (Say pee-nuh-CAH-tay. It's Spanish.)

Now, javelinas stink all the time, but pinacate beetles stink only for special occasions. When something's bugging them!

If a predator bothers a pinacate beetle, the beetle doesn't smell bad right away. First it just points its rear end up in the air. WARNING: stay away—or else!

Then if the predator doesn't get the message, the beetle squirts disgusting smelly brown goop out of its rear end. **YUCK!** If that predator is smart, he'll never bug a pinacate beetle again!

And if you're smart, *you* won't bug one of those little stinkers either!

Lots of people think dead rattlesnakes can bite.

What do *you* think?
FACT or CACTIFRACT?

If you said FACT, yup,
YOU'RE BRAINIER THAN A BUZZWORM!

Know what a reflex is? It's a movement your body makes without your brain having to think about it. When the doctor bonks your knee with a rubber hammer and your leg kicks, that's a reflex. It's automatic!

Ready for the spooky part?

A rattler has reflexes, too. Some of those reflexes can still work for a while after a rattlesnake dies—even though its brain has stopped working! Its body can still wiggle around. Its mouth can still open. Venom can still squirt out of its fangs! **YOW!**

Never touch a dead rattlesnake. (Or a live one, either!)

Lots of people think hummingbirds migrate on the backs of geese.

What do *you* think?
FACT or CACTIFRACT?

If you said CACTIFRACT, CORRECTO, AMIGO!

But what a great idea! Just imagine. Where would the goose airports be? Would the hummingbirds wear seat belts? Where would they put their luggage?

Actually, hummingbirds don't need any help going wherever they want. Hummingbirds are fantastic flyers. Terrific travelers, too!

Most hummingbirds in the desert migrate every year. Many kinds buzz over to the desert, hang around a few months, then zip off again to far-away places. See you next year! Other kinds only stop by in the desert on their way someplace else. Can't stay, gotta go!

If you're out birdwatching and you see hummingbirds on a goose's back, what should you do? Get better binoculars right away!

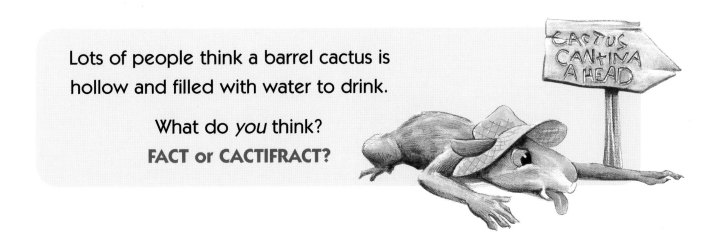

Lots of people think a barrel cactus is hollow and filled with water to drink.

What do *you* think?
FACT or CACTIFRACT?

If you said CACTIFRACT, bingo!
YOU WIN ONE CACTILLION DOLLARS!

A barrel cactus isn't hollow at all! It's filled with spongy stuff. Like the sponge in your kitchen, the stuff inside the cactus can hold water. Cactus sponge water! Sound good?

Long ago, very thirsty travelers sometimes chopped the top right off a barrel cactus. (Watch out! Dangerous spines!) Then they pounded and pounded the spongy insides with a giant stick, to squish out a little cactus juice.

Hard work! And the juice they got was all slimy and gross.

Always bring plenty of water with you in the desert. It won't be slimy! And opening a canteen is a *lot* easier than opening a cactus!

Lots of people think female black widow spiders eat their mates.

What do *you* think?
FACT or CACTIFRACT?

If you said FACT,
STUPENDOUS, AMAZING SPIDERKID!

The male black widow spider has a **BIG** problem. It's the female! Compared to him, she's huge!

When the male is ready to mate, he comes up to the female very carefully. He jiggles her web in a special way, to let her know he's not just another tasty fly! Then—if he's lucky—she'll let him mate with her.

But then things get *really* dangerous. Sometimes he gets away safely. Whoa—that was close! But more often the female catches him, sinks her fangs into him, and squirts venom into his body. Then she sucks out his insides!

The moral? If you're a male black widow spider, don't hang around for supper. *You* might be the main course!

Lots of people think if you leave your watch outside at night, a packrat might leave some cactus in its place.

What do *you* think? **FACT or CACTIFRACT?**

If you said FACT, partner...
CORRECTAMUNDO!

A packrat might also leave cactus in place of your toothbrush—or your best action figure! But he's not trying to make a fair trade.

A packrat piles up cactus bits and other weird stuff to make his house. He scampers around at night to find what he needs.

Now imagine one night you leave your watch on the ground next to your sleeping bag. Big mistake number one!

While you're asleep, along comes you know who, carrying a piece of cactus for his house. He spots something sparkling in the moonlight. Your watch! It's *way* cooler than cactus! He drops the cactus right there and takes your watch home instead.

Now for big mistake number two. The next morning you reach for your watch without looking!

 **Oops—time to go!**

Some people might think it's easy to tell
a FACT from a CACTIFRACT.

What do *you* think? How many did you get right?

Adios!

MORE EXTRA BONUS WEIRD STUFF ABSOLUTELY FREE!

Want to find out more about the critters in this book?
Visit the Arizona-Sonora Desert Museum's website! **www.desertmuseum.org**
When you get there, type a *secret code word* in the SEARCH box, then click on the SEARCH button.
What secret code word? You'll figure it out!

DESERT TORTOISE

Danger! A baby tortoise's shell hardly protects it at all from hungry predators like coyotes and ravens. How come? *TORTAMUNDO*

GILA MONSTER

There are only two kinds of venomous lizards on planet Earth. Our friend the Gila monster is one. What's the other, and where in the world does *it* live? *CHOMPAMUNDO*

HORNY TOAD

Squirt gun eyes work great against members of the dog family. But how does a horny toad protect itself from all the other critters that want it for lunch? *SQUIRTAMUNDO*

JUMPING CACTUS

Oh no! You backed up without looking first, and now a piece of jumping cactus is stuck to you where it really hurts! Quick—what should you do about it? *OUCHAMUNDO*

JAVELINA

Javelinas smell *really terrible,* but no one has ever seen a javelina holding its nose. Can javelinas smell each other? *STINKAMUNDO*

PINACATE BEETLE

The cool Spanish word **pinacate** comes from **pinacatl**, a word in an ancient Mexican language. Wonder what **pinacatl** means? Take a guess! *BUGAMUNDO*

RATTLESNAKE

How long do you think a dead rattlesnake is dangerous? A minute? A day? Longer than it takes to say "brainier than a buzzworm"? Find out! *BUZZAMUNDO*

HUMMINGBIRD

OK, so a hummer doesn't have to hop on a goose to get where it's going. But how far can a mini-bird like that fly all by itself? You might be surprised! *HUMMAMUNDO*

BARREL CACTUS

Even if you just *love* drinking stuff that's slimy and gross, you should never try getting juice from a barrel cactus! Why not? *YUCKAMUNDO*

BLACK WIDOW SPIDER

More black widow spiders live around buildings than out in the wild desert. Some might be living at *your* house right now! How scared should you be? *YIKESAMUNDO*

PACKRAT

A packrat's house looks like a big messy pile of stuff on the outside, but on the inside it's pretty awesome! Want to know why? *COOLAMUNDO*

Can you say
FACT or CACTIFRACT
ten times really fast?

About the Author

David Lazaroff got interested in nature when he was a boy in California, catching frogs and lizards after school. Now he lives in Tucson, Arizona, where he writes books about nature and takes nature photos. He still thinks frogs and lizards are extremely cool.

Some other books David has written are *Sabino Canyon, The Secret Lives of Hummingbirds,* and *Arizona-Sonora Desert Museum Book of Answers.* This is his first book for kids.

About the Illustrator

Preston Neel was born in Macon, Georgia in 1959. He studied for three years at the Academy of Art College in San Francisco, California. When Preston was a boy he loved books by Dr. Seuss and by P. D. Eastman. He hopes his books will inspire children the way those books inspired him.

Some other children's books Preston has illustrated are *Frank the Fish Gets His Wish, Roadrunners and Sandwich Terns,* and *Tumblebugs and Hairy Bears.*

About Prickly Pete

Prickly Pete is a packrat with a stylish hat. He grew up in the desert, but only he knows exactly where. If you go exploring in the desert, look for his house. It's the one with the space captain action figure on the roof.

Prickly Pete has never been in a book before, but once, before he knew better, he chewed on one.